Sly the Sleuth

Sly the Sleuth

and the Code Mysteries

by Donna Jo Napoli and Robert Furrow

illustrated by Heather Maione

Dial Books for Young Readers

DIAL BOOKS FOR YOUNG READERS
A division of Penguin Young Readers Group
Published by The Penguin Group
Penguin Group (USA) Inc., 375 Hudson Street, New York, NY 10014, U.S.A.
Penguin Group (Canada), 90 Eglinton Avenue East, Suite 700, Toronto, Ontario, Canada
M4P 2Y3 (a division of Pearson Penguin Canada Inc.)
Penguin Books Ltd, 80 Strand, London WC2R 0RL, England
Penguin Ireland, 25 St. Stephen's Green, Dublin 2, Ireland
(a division of Penguin Books Ltd)
Penguin Group (Australia), 250 Camberwell Road, Camberwell, Victoria 3124, Australia
(a division of Pearson Australia Group Pty Ltd)
Penguin Books India Pvt Ltd, 11 Community Centre,
Panchsheel Park, New Delhi - 110 017, India
Penguin Group (NZ), 67 Apollo Drive, Rosedale, North Shore 0623,
New Zealand (a division of Pearson New Zealand Ltd)
Penguin Books (South Africa) (Pty) Ltd, 24 Sturdee Avenue, Rosebank,
Johannesburg 2196, South Africa
Penguin Books Ltd, Registered Offices: 80 Strand, London WC2R 0RL, England
Text copyright © 2009 by Donna Jo Napoli and Robert Furrow
Illustrations copyright © 2009 by Heather Maione
Designed by Jasmin Rubero
Text set in Bembo
Printed in the U.S.A.
1   3   5   7   9   10   8   6   4   2
Library of Congress Cataloging-in-Publication Data
Napoli, Donna Jo, date.
Sly the sleuth and the code mysteries / by Donna Jo Napoli and Robert
Furrow ; illustrated by Heather Maione.
p.   cm.
Summary: Sly uses her detective skills to help her friends solve
mysteries that all involve some kind of code.
ISBN 978-0-8037-3345-9
[1. Ciphers—Fiction. 2. Mystery and detective stories.] I. Furrow, Robert, date.
II. Maione, Heather Harms, ill. III. Title.
PZ7.N15Sj 2009
[Fic]—dc22
2008018439

For Baci and Ino
—D.J.N and R.F.

For my mom—love you!!!!
–H.M.

Sly the Sleuth

and the Code Mysteries

Case #1:

Sly and the Song Beat

Out of Here

It was Sunday afternoon. The perfect time to work. I searched the shelf. There it was: *Best Desserts Ever*. I carried the book to the kitchen table.

Shuuuu—the porch door opened. *Shuuuup*— it closed. "Brian?" I called. Brian is my neighbor. He's only four. He never knocks.

Brian waddled in. Brian is skinny. But in that snowsuit he looked fat.

His hood was up. A scarf covered his nose and mouth.

"*Gghrkrrn,*" said Brian.

I unwound his scarf. "Speak, Brian."

"YouTube."

That didn't sound like the mumble before. Besides, Brian probably didn't know what YouTube was. "What did you say?"

"Where's your computer?"

Brian's mom doesn't even allow TV. "Does your mom really let you go to YouTube?"

Brian didn't say anything.

I was glad he wasn't a liar.

I opened the book.

4

Brian peeked around me. "I love to cook."

"This is important, Brian."

"Is it a case?"

I run a detective agency: Sleuth for Hire. I'm Sly the sleuth. "Not really," I said. "Just a favor."

"I cook good."

"Forget it, Brian."

"You won't let me have any fun," said Brian. "You stink. Get with the program, Sly."

"What?" I blinked at him. "What did you just say?"

"I'm out of here." Brian waddled toward the door.

Out of here? "Who taught you to talk like that?"

Brian turned around. "Tattletales are bad."

Hopeful

I raised an eyebrow. My father taught me that. Sleuths do it. "What's going on, Brian?"

Brian put his hands over his mouth. His mittens almost covered his face.

"Come on, Brian, tell."

"No."

This was odd. Brian always wanted to tell me everything. "Come back. I think you can help me after all."

Brian waddled over.

I looked in the book index.

He panted in my ear.

"What's the matter, Brian?"

"I can't breathe." His face was bright and sweaty.

I helped Brian take off his snowsuit and mittens.

Knock-knock-knock. Shuuuu. Shuuuup. That meant Melody was here. Melody is my best friend. She always knocks. But she never waits for an answer.

"Hi, Sly. Hi, Brian." Melody hung her jacket over a chair. She picked up Brian's snowsuit. She hung it over a chair. Melody is neat. "Why is your door making that funny noise?"

"My father put something on the bottom. To keep out the cold."

"Oh. That's smart. Let's do something fun."

"I'm busy," I said.

Melody looked at Brian. She looked at me. "It's a good day for painting."

"I love to paint," said Brian.

Melody knew that. Everyone knew Brian loved to paint.

I glared at Melody. "I'm busy."

"Can't it wait?" said Melody. "I'm your best friend."

"I love to paint," said Brian.

"He loves to paint," said Melody.

Ganging up isn't nice.

7

But Brian looked hopeful.

So did Melody.

Melody was right. It could wait.

Art

We went to the porch. I spread newspaper on the floor. My mother says art projects with Brian must be on the floor. Brian knocks things over. This way they don't fall far. And they don't splatter far.

I got the paint set. And the brushes. And a bowl of water. And three sheets of paper.

I sat on the newspaper. Brian sat on one side of me. Melody sat on the other.

We made a circle. It felt cozy. Painting was a good idea. I smiled at Melody.

We painted a long time.

Melody looked over at Brian's paper. "That's nice."

It was a dinosaur. Like always. But this wasn't a T. rex. It had a long neck. And a round body. Brontosaurus?

"Are you going to add squares?" asked Melody.

"What?" said Brian.

"You know. Giraffe skin has squares. Up and down the neck and on the back and everywhere. Everywhere but the belly, I think."

Giraffe? I blinked at Brian's painting.

Brian blinked at his painting.

"You don't have to," said Melody. "It's up to you. It's your giraffe."

"I love giraffes," said Brian.

"It shows," said Melody. "You draw them good."

Brian pointed at Melody. "You're the bomb." He crawled across the newspaper and kissed her on the cheek.

He knocked over the bowl of water.

"Uh-oh," I said. "Your painting's ruined, Melody."

"It doesn't matter." Melody took another piece of paper. She smiled at Brian.

He smiled back. "You should work at my school. You should be an art teacher."

My cheeks burned. I did art with Brian all the time. He never said *I* should be an art teacher.

Noah

The phone rang. "Hello?"

"Don't say my name, Sly. I don't want Brian to know it's me."

Mrs. Olsen? "Okay."

"Please observe him."

"Anything special?"

"Just observe him. I'll talk to you later."

"Okay."

"Thank you. Bye now."

I went back to the porch.

I observed Brian. He was painting.

Thud. Thud-thud.

I knew that sound.

Brian looked at me. "Jack!" shouted Brian. He ran to the door.

Jack always kicked his soccer ball against the door.

Brian opened the door.

Noah came in. With the wind.

Taxi, my cat, yowled.

"Where's Jack?" asked Brian.

Noah shrugged.

I picked up Taxi and hugged her. Her paws were cold.

Brian reached up and petted Taxi on the top of her head. She loves that best.

"You've been around Jack too much," I said to Noah. "You knock just like him."

Melody giggled. "Well, of course. He lives with him."

Noah is Jack's cousin. He came to visit and wound up staying.

Noah looked at our paintings. Then he looked at me.

I got the message.

"Okay, Melody and Brian. Time to go. I have business with Noah."

"Oh," said Melody. "Is Noah a case?"

"People are clients. Not cases."

"Is he a client?" said Melody.

"No. We have to cook now," I said. "See you later."

"I cook good," said Brian. "Marissa loves soup."

Marissa was Brian's new babysitter. I hadn't

met her yet. She came two afternoons a week. Marissa wouldn't let Brian cook. Not unless she was crazy. "Go home, Brian."

I set Taxi down. I held out Brian's snowsuit.

He smushed it into a ball. "Who needs a snowsuit?"

This was a good question. Brian lived next door. A jacket would do. But last week Mrs. Olsen told me he needed to wear that snowsuit. She was firm.

"I'll help you."

"Get with the program, Sly." Brian ran out the door.

Melody followed.

Noah looked at me with a question on his face.

I shrugged. After all, that was Noah's language.

cake

Noah raised his eyebrows. Both of them. He wasn't a sleuth. He was just asking a question.

I led Noah to the kitchen. I checked the book index again. I opened to the right page.

Noah looked at the recipe. He looked at me.

I nodded.

I got out butter, sugar, chocolate chips, cocoa powder, and eggs. I put everything in front of Noah.

Noah mixed up the sugar, cocoa powder, and eggs.

I melted the butter and the chocolate chips. I poured it into Noah's bowl.

Noah stirred.

I buttered the pan.

Noah poured in the batter.

I put it in the oven.

Noah turned on the oven to 350 degrees. He was a good partner. He knew how to do his part.

We sat down at the table.

Noah took out an iPod. He looked at me.

I looked at him.

He put an earbud in his ear. He gave me the other earbud.

I put it in my ear.

We listened to rap. I don't like rap. I wanted to read a book. But maybe Noah would feed bad.

After a while, Noah turned off the iPod. "Are you sure this will work?"

I flinched. It was a shock to hear so many words from Noah.

"Princess loves chocolate. And this cake has no flour. So she won't be allergic to it."

Noah just looked at me. He was right. I hadn't answered his question.

Noah wanted Princess to like him. So he was making her food. He got the idea from Jack. Jack wanted Melody to like him. He had been secretly leaving oranges in her cubby. Both of them were nuts.

Noah stared at me now. His eyes asked: Will it work?

Who could say? In life, you take your chances. But I like to be upbeat. "If it doesn't work, we'll try something else."

Half an hour later, we wrapped the chocolate cake in tin foil.

Noah carried it out the door.

And there was Mrs. Olsen. Just about to knock.

MRI

"Sly, dear." Mrs. Olsen came in. She shut the porch door. *Shuuuup.* "Weather-stripping. Hmmm. I'll have to try that." She turned to me with a hummph. "I'm upset, dear."

Mrs. Olsen had never called me dear before. Now she said it twice. She must be mad at me. Brian didn't wear his snowsuit home. And I didn't observe him for long. "I'm sorry."

Mrs. Olsen looked surprised. "Whatever for?"

Dumb me, that clearly wasn't why she was here. "Would you like a glass of cider, Mrs. Olsen?"

"What a nice offer. But I can't leave Brian alone that long. You know how strange he's been."

"Strange?"

"You don't have to hide things from me, Sly. Brian's been strange." Mrs. Olsen's face crumpled. She looked like she might cry.

"You mean the way he talks?"

"So he does it with you too." A tear slid down Mrs. Olsen's cheek. "That's what I needed to know. Whether he does it all the time. Oh, dear."

Brian said he was "out of here." He told Melody she was "the bomb." He said "Get with the program." Twice. That's how big kids talked. It was strange for a four-year-old. But it was nothing to cry about. "It's not that bad."

"We're going to the doctor on Friday."

"The doctor? Because of how Brian talks?"

"I bet he'll schedule an MRI."

"What's an MRI?"

"Something that sees inside your head. Brian might have a brain problem."

Pressure on the Brain

I sat down on the floor. I just dropped. My whole body went cold. "What do you mean?"

Mrs. Olsen squatted. She closed her arms around her knees. She looked small and sad. "I've been on the Internet. It's helpful. Without it, waiting to go to the doctor would drive me crazy."

I understood. Waiting for her to explain was driving me crazy.

"The way Brian talks is called dysprosody. Pressure on the brain causes it."

Mrs. Olsen made no sense. I stared at her.

"It gives him that funny singsong."

"What singsong?" I said.

"Like he's speaking with a foreign accent."

"Brian doesn't sound foreign."

"Well, he doesn't sound normal."

I don't like to tell adults they are wrong. But

this was important. "Some people talk like that."

"Don't be silly, Sly. No one says what Brian says."

"Big kids do. He must have learned it from someone."

Mrs. Olsen stood up. She put her hand to her mouth. "I wish you were right." She looked at me hard. "All right, Sly. I'm hiring you. Find out whether Brian learned this from someone."

"Why not ask him yourself?"

"I did. He told me not to spy on him."

"Were you spying on him?"

"Not at first. I simply overheard him. But after that, I listened on purpose. I was worried, you see."

I did see. Anyone could see how worried Mrs. Olsen was.

Mrs. Olsen leaned over me. "Please, Sly?"

I take only fun cases. And cases Taxi would like. Taxi is my case buddy. Every sleuth needs a buddy to talk to.

This case did not sound fun. But it was about Brian. Brian knew how to pet cats right. Taxi would take this case. Probably any cat would.

Besides, I loved Brian.

I went into the kitchen. I got my sharpest pencil. I got my special pad of paper. These were tools of the trade. I marched back to Mrs. Olsen. "Let's go."

Bad Words

Mrs. Olsen stopped outside Brian's room. She put her ear to the door. "Listen."

Spying. And now eavesdropping. None of this was nice. "Stand back," I said to Mrs. Olsen.

"Stand back?" she said weakly.

"Leave this to me. After all, you hired me."

"Well, all right, Sly."

"You can go do something else now," I said.

"I guess I'll make some cookies. For you." She brightened. "I'll get a head start on your payment."

Mrs. Olsen paid me in cookies. Mrs. Olsen is a health nut. Her cookies use whole wheat and flax seed. The last time she paid me, I gave the cookies to Jack. He used them as pucks for his shuffleboard game. "Thank you," I said. Sleuths must be polite. My father says that's good business. Plus, I don't like to be rude.

I knocked on Brian's door.

No one answered.

I knocked harder.

No one answered.

I opened the door.

Brian's back was to me. He was jumping on the bed. And talking. Loudly. In something like a chant. "Bin BART bees bo BUpid be BAKES ba bool BINK."

"Brian?" I said.

He stopped jumping and turned around.

"Brian, what are you doing?"

"Binging."

"I don't understand."

"Bats bite."

I gulped. "Brian, did a bat bite you?"

He laughed. "Bore bunny."

"Can you talk to me regular?"

"Sure."

I was so relieved, I hugged myself. "You have to tell me. Did a bat bite you?"

"No."

"Then why were you saying those things?"

"I'm mad."

"Who are you mad at?"

"Amanda."

"Who's Amanda?"

"She's at my school." Brian goes to nursery school.

"Why are you mad at her?"

"She doesn't like anything I do."

"Does she speak weird too?"

Brian laughed. "You're funny, Sly." He bounced onto his bottom. "Amanda yells."

I might get mad at Amanda too.

"I hate Monday."

What did Monday have to do with anything? But I had other things to find out. "Who taught you to speak like that?"

"Tattletales are bad."

All right. Sleuths know how to change tack. "What do those strange things mean?"

"My mother doesn't like bad words."

Were those bad words in disguise? I took out my pad of paper. "Please say them again."

"I'm not done."

"What do you mean?"

"Only the third line, okay?" said Brian.

"Line?"

Brian got to his feet again. He jumped and chanted.

I wrote.

B

At recess on Monday I walked off alone. I took out my pad of paper. I looked at Brian's words. "Bin bart bees bo bupid be bakes ba bool bink."

This was a code, for sure. A "b" code. I smiled. "B" for "Brian." It made sense.

But how did the code work? When I asked if a bat had bitten him, he laughed. He said, "Bore bunny." Brian's always telling me I'm funny. And *bore bunny* rhymes with *you're funny*. Oh. Maybe Brian substituted the "b" sound for the beginning of every word.

I read Brian's words again. Out loud this time. I said each one slowly. "Bin bart bees bo bupid be bakes ba bool bink."

"I didn't know you were that religion."

I turned around.

Jack stood there. Noah was right behind him.

"What religion?"

"The one that talks like that. My uncle told me all about it," said Jack. "It's called speaking in tongues. Do you roll on the floor too?"

"This isn't speaking in tongues," I said.

"It sounds like it."

"Well, it's not. It's a code."

"For what?"

I had no idea yet. But clients lose confidence in sleuths who have no idea. And both Jack and Noah could be future clients. "I can't say."

"Oh, it's a case, huh? Cool." Jack punched Noah in the shoulder. Noah punched Jack back. I don't know why they do that. "Is it dangerous?"

"You might be better off staying at a distance," I said.

Jack backed away. He turned and left.

"Have you given Princess the cake yet?" I asked Noah.

Noah shook his head. He put on his iPod earbuds. He hurried after Jack. But with a funny swing to his shoulders. There was something familiar about it.

I looked down at the pad of paper. I said the words again. But this time I said them like Brian said them. Fast, and with a beat. "Bin BART bees bo BUpid be BAKES ba bool BINK."

Brian had called this a line. Like in a song. And he told me he was binging—which must mean singing.

28

There was no doubt about it. Brian was singing with a really strong rhythm. He didn't have a brain problem.

The case was solved.

But Brian still wasn't happy. He was mad.

I needed to know what Brian was singing. Brian was smart. Putting "b" for the beginning of every word was a hard code to crack.

Real Words

I went straight to Brian's house after school. I knocked on the back door. No one answered. I tried the knob. It was open.

No one was in the kitchen. The stove was dirty. A chair was pushed in front of it. A short person could reach the stove from that chair.

Brian was short. He had said he cooked good. And he said Marissa loved soup.

Maybe Marissa was crazy after all.

I walked into the living room.

Rap music came from upstairs. I knew that rhythm. That was the same rhythm that Brian used in his singing. I followed it. To the family room.

Brian was dancing. A teenager with long curly hair was dancing. The music came from the computer. From a YouTube video.

"Hi, Sly!" Brian grinned. Then his face fell. He ran to the computer and turned it off.

The girl stopped dancing. Her mouth hung open. "Hello, Sly. Nice to meet you. I'm Marissa."

"I figured."

"Tattletales are bad," said Brian.

Marissa put on a big fake smile. "Brian talks about you all the time. You're the bomb."

Oh yeah? I thought Melody was the bomb. "Brian, do you listen to this music a lot?"

"Tattletales are bad."

What was bad was some rap words. At least

for four-year-olds. "Sing me your favorite words."

"Ba BUM ba ba BUM ba ba BUM ba ba BUM."

"No, I mean real words."

"Ba CAT ba ba RAT ba ba DOWN ba ba ROUND."

It looked like Brian just caught the beat, not the words. Good. This was okay rapping for a four-year-old.

"Well . . ." Marissa bit her bottom lip. "Oh, I know. Brian, why don't you show Sly what you made in art today?"

Brian ran to his room. We followed. He held up a clay animal.

Marissa nodded. "It's a—"

"Giraffe," I said. "It's good, Brian."

Brian beamed.

"So Brian, have you finished writing your rap?" I said.

"It's good."

"Can I hear it? But the 'b' way, please." I took out my pad of paper.

Brian climbed on his bed and jumped as he rapped.

BaMANda biz BAD buzz be BELLS band be BELLS

Be BATES by biRAFFE band be BELLS band be BELLS

Bin BART bees bo BUpid be BAKES ba bool BINK

Ba BINK ba big BINK ba bat BINK ba bink BINK

"Hey, that's really hot, Brian," said Marissa. "What does it mean?"

"No, don't tell," I said. "I want to figure it out."

Decoding

I put Brian's rap on the kitchen table and stared at it.

> Bamanda biz bad buzz be
> bells band be bells
> Be bates by biraffe band
> be bells band be bells
> Bin bart bees bo bupid be
> bakes ba bool bink
> Ba bink ba big bink ba
> bat bink ba bink bink

Then I wrote down everything I knew about this case. Brian was mad at Amanda. And Amanda was at school. And Amanda yells. And Brian made a giraffe today. So I looked for the words *Amanda, school, yells,* and *giraffe.* And one word was obvious: *bupid* had to be *stupid.*

> AMANDA biz bad buzz be
> YELLS band be YELLS
> Be bates by GIRAFFE

band be YELLS band be
YELLS

Bin bart bees bo STUPID
be bakes ba SCHOOL bink

Ba bink ba big bink ba
bat bink ba bink bink

Bink came up a lot. And Brian said there
were bad words in this rap. And when Brian
was mad at me on Sunday, he said I stink. Mrs.
Olsen probably thinks *stink* is a bad word. So
bink must be *stink*.

AMANDA biz bad buzz be
YELLS band be YELLS

Be bates by GIRAFFE
band be YELLS band be
YELLS

Bin bart bees bo STUPID
be bakes ba SCHOOL STINK

Ba STINK ba big STINK
ba bat STINK ba STINK
STINK

Big was a real word—and even though it had many other words that rhymed with it, I was pretty sure *big* meant "big" because the *ba* in front of it rhymed with *a*. So that would make "a big stink." In fact, all the *ba*'s in the last line were probably *a*'s. And *band* might just be *and*. And Brian thinks Amanda is bad. And that's what the first three words rhyme with.

> AMANDA IS BAD buzz be
> YELLS AND be YELLS
>   Be bates by GIRAFFE
> AND be YELLS AND be
> YELLS
>   Bin bart bees bo STUPID
> be bakes ba SCHOOL STINK
>   A STINK A BIG STINK A
> bat STINK A STINK STINK

Hmm. This was starting to make sense. I was pretty sure *be* was *she*. And *bo* in front of *stupid* was probably *so*. And *by* in front of *giraffe* could be *my*.

AMANDA IS BAD buzz
SHE YELLS AND SHE YELLS
SHE bates MY GIRAFFE
AND SHE YELLS AND SHE
YELLS
Bin bart bees SO STUPID
SHE bakes ba SCHOOL
STINK
A STINK A BIG STINK A
bat STINK A STINK STINK

Good. But some things were still too hard. I had no clue what *bin bart bees* meant. And what rhymed with *bat* that made sense with *stink*?

I picked up the telephone. I dialed.

"Hello?"

"Hello, Mrs. Olsen. This is Sly."

"Oh, Sly. Do you have an answer for me already?"

"Sort of. Do you know the kids in Brian's class?"

"Some of them."

"Can you tell me about Amanda?"

"Amanda? Who's that? Wait just a moment while I check the class list." A few seconds later Mrs. Olsen said, "I was right. There's no Amanda."

"Are you sure? Brian talked about Amanda."

"Well, none of the kids are called Amanda. None of the teachers either. Although we do have a substitute in art now. The real teacher had a baby. But I don't know her name."

Art! "I bet Brian doesn't like the new art teacher, does he?"

"How did you guess? He says she hates his clay work. You know how Brian talks. Last week she didn't give him a star for his bowl. And this week she didn't give him a star for his giraffe. He doesn't like her at all."

"Is Brian still awake?"

"Yes."

"I'll come over in a minute. Bye, Mrs. Olsen."

I took one last swipe at it:

AMANDA IS BAD 'CAUSE
SHE YELLS AND SHE YELLS
 SHE HATES MY GIRAFFE
AND SHE YELLS AND SHE
YELLS
 IN ART SHE'S SO STUPID
SHE MAKES THE SCHOOL
STINK
 A STINK A BIG STINK
A RAT STINK A STINK
STINK

'Cause certainly made sense for *buzz*. *Rat* wasn't great, but it was better than *bat*.

Our Rap

It turned out I'd made a few mistakes. Here's how Brian's rap really went:

> *Amanda is bad 'cause she yells and she yells*
> *She hates my giraffe and she smells and she smells*
> *In art she's so stupid she makes the school stink*
> *A stink a big stink a fat stink a stink stink*

My mistakes were understandable. After all, lots of words rhyme.

Brian was healthy. Mrs. Olsen was happy to learn that. Brian listened to rap. Mrs. Olsen was not happy to learn that. But she felt better that Brian didn't understand the words to most rap songs. And she agreed that Brian's rap was pretty good for a four-year-old.

Marissa loved YouTube. But she guessed

that Mrs. Olsen wouldn't want Brian to watch. That's why she told him tattletales are bad. She was scared when I caught them watching YouTube. But she got happy again, because Mrs. Olsen didn't fire her. Now Marissa has two strict rules. No YouTube. No teen rap. But she could dance with Brian to other music. Mrs. Olsen thought dancing was good. There was a third rule too: Brian couldn't cook alone. But he could cook with Marissa.

Amanda would be art teacher for only one more week. Brian was happy to learn that.

And Jack was happy. Jack was not part of this case. But Mrs. Olsen paid me in cookies. And I gave the cookies to Jack. So Jack is planning a shuffleboard party next weekend.

This was my first code mystery. It went fine. Figuring out codes is exciting. Plus I like rap now. Not the kind that talks about people beating up on people. But the funny kind, for kids. I found a website full of great raps. Even

Mrs. Olsen agrees. So Brian is allowed to listen with me. Not with Marissa.

We made our own rap.

A mother gets happy to know her kid's smart

A kid gets to smile and enjoy all his art

A teen keeps her job and she's fun, which is good

And Sly solved the case as a sleuth always should

Case #2:

Sly and the Word Beat

Gibberish

I threw my stuff in my cubby. In a rush. Baseball practice started today.

I love baseball. I catch bad. I pitch bad. I run bad. But I still love it.

I have to be at every practice. That way Coach won't cut me. Any coach feels guilty to cut someone who comes to every practice.

Through the windows I looked out on snow. Just a couple of inches. But the sky was dark. It might dump more.

Practice was indoors. So we didn't bring

45

mitts. Too bad. A mitt felt good on my hand. I loped toward the gym.

"Hey, Sly, wait up." Melody came running.

"No time," I said. "Base—"

"Ball practice," said Melody. "That's all you've been talking about for a week. But I got a note again."

I slowed down. Melody got a strange note on Friday. Someone left it in her cubby. Without a name. The note made no sense. She threw it out. "Does it make sense?"

"No," said Melody.

"Does it have a name?"

"No."

I ran again. "Throw it out," I called over my shoulder.

Melody ran behind me. "This one is spelled right. I could read it."

I stopped. "What does it say?"

"Look." She held it out.

Someone snatched it from behind. Kate!

She's so nosy. "It's gibberish. Throw it out."
She's also bossy.

"Do you think the person is saying I'm a
dove?" Melody asked Kate. "That would be
nice, right? Is that what it means?"

This was a strange question. Too bad I was
in a hurry.

"I have no idea what it means," said Kate.
"Neither does the person who wrote it. See
all those question marks? That means the person has no idea of anything."

"Case solved," I said, even though this wasn't

a case. Sleuths talk like that. And it's important to remind people I'm the sleuth. Kate doesn't know anything about sleuthing. "Got to run."

Practice

Indoor practice was divided into four stations.

Coach set up two portable nets in one corner. That station was for pitching.

Coach brought Wiffle balls and set up a tee in another corner. That station was for batting.

The third station was soft toss—just tossing Wiffle balls back and forth.

The last station was agility training.

Coach divided us into four groups. I got to be with Emily and Chaundra and Jeff and Orson. Each group went to a station. Every five minutes Coach blew his whistle. That meant change stations.

It was great. I got hit in the face only once. And Wiffle balls don't hurt. I walked home tired and happy.

Princess was walking along the other sidewalk. A girl was with her. I'd never seen her before. Their arms were hooked. Princess likes to hook arms. Her family does that.

"Hey, Princess." I waved.

Princess smiled and waved back. Her teeth were clean. No chocolate. Noah must not have given her the cake yet.

She said something to the girl. Then she crossed the street alone. "Were you at baseball practice?"

"Yes," I said.

"I wasn't."

Well, I knew that. "Who's your friend?"

"My cousin. My aunt brought her here for two whole weeks."

"Doesn't she have school?"

"Yeah. But my aunt wanted to come."

"Can I meet her?"

"She's shy. You wouldn't like her anyway. She complains. She hates the snow. And the dark. And she's homesick. All she wants to do is eat pizza. Anyway, after she leaves I'll come to baseball practice."

This was a switch. Princess didn't play team sports. "Are you good at it?"

"I don't know."

"Have you ever played before?"

"No."

Uh-oh. Princess had no chance unless she was a pity case. Like me. "Listen, Princess. You'd better come to practice tomorrow. Coach is strict."

"I have to play with Lucia after school."

"Every day?"

"I can't leave Lucia all lonesome. Mamma says."

I understood. I have a mother too. Poor Princess. She'd never make the team.

Best Friends

I cut across Melody's yard. In the back was a hedge. I squirmed through. Now I was in Brian's backyard. Snow sat thinly on the branches of his apple tree. Even on the skinny branches. It made a glowing white outline.

Winter was pretty.

It's too bad Princess's cousin didn't like it.

I kicked through the powder. Someone else had left prints in the snow. They went to my porch door.

Melody sat on the step. "It took you long enough," she said.

"You're sure grumpy."

"What do you expect? You're supposed to be my best friend, not Kate."

"What did Kate do?"

"Nothing. She just walked me home. And talked my head off. It's what you did."

"What did I do?"

"Nothing."

"You're not making sense, Melody."

"You did nothing. That's the problem. I get wacky notes and you don't even care."

"I care."

"You wouldn't care if I froze on this step. You wouldn't care if you never saw me again." Melody's head drooped. It landed on her knees.

This was too dramatic, even for Melody.

"Are you still rehearsing for the spring play tryouts?"

"Yes. How did you know?"

"Just a guess."

Melody sat up tall. "Are you being sarcastic? Because sarcasm isn't nice."

"Sorry."

"At least I got another orange. That means someone likes me. Even if I do know it's just Princess."

Those were the oranges Jack left. But I was sworn to secrecy. "Why do you think the oranges are from Princess?"

"They're red inside. Blood oranges. The kind her father grows in their sunroom."

I didn't answer.

"You know, the kind from Sicily."

"Maybe they are from Princess's sunroom. But that doesn't mean she gave them to you."

"Don't be dumb. Who else would give me oranges from her sunroom?"

Jack helped Princess's father take care of the orange trees. Melody knew that.

Princess's father paid Jack in oranges. Melody didn't know that.

I looked away so Melody couldn't see my face. Keeping a secret from your best friend isn't easy.

"Okay, Sly. Tell me the truth."

I turned back to her. Please don't make me, I wished.

Melody's face was sad. "Do you think I'm dishonest?"

"What? Not at all."

"But when people con other people, that means they fool them. Right? So if you con people, you're dishonest."

"Who conned anyone?"

"Someone is thinking bad things about me. Read this note." Melody held it out.

I read:

Pizza?

Con me?

Dove?

"It makes no sense, Melody."

Melody chewed on the side of her thumb. "It's awful to get an anonymous note. It's creepy."

It felt creepy to me too. "You are not a pizza. You are not a dove. And you don't con any-one." I put my arm around Melody. "Forget this note. Whoever wrote it is crazy."

"How do you know?"

"I'm your best friend."

Cubby Watch

It was 3:12. I cleared off my desk.

Then 3:13. I put on my backpack.

Then 3:14. I stood in the aisle.

The bell rang. I dashed out the door. I ran to the hall where Melody's cubby was.

No one was at the cubbies yet. Good. If anyone came, I would see. I would find out who the crazy note-writer was.

Melody didn't ask me to take her case. Best friends don't have to ask.

And cats are loyal. Taxi understands friendship. She'd want me to take this case. Probably any cat would.

I leaned against the wall. I hummed. That way I looked inconspicuous. It's a sleuth trick.

People were slow getting to their cubbies. And I was in a hurry. Baseball practice was starting. Hurry up, people, I said inside my head. Hurry, hurry, hurry.

Princess came down the hall.

I looked at my shoes. I watched her out of the corner of my eye.

Princess went toward Melody's cubby. My heart thumped. Princess didn't seem crazy.

But you never know. Sleuths have to be ready for surprises.

Princess stopped at the cubby before Melody's. She took stuff out. Then she looked my way. "Hey, Sly. Aren't you going to baseball practice?"

"Of course I am. Are you coming after all?"

She shook her head. "My cousin's waiting. See you later."

By now lots of kids were at their cubbies. But no one went to Melody's cubby.

Except Melody. She saw me. "What are you doing here?"

"Nothing," I said.

"You're watching my cubby, aren't you? You're watching for the mystery person. You think this is a case. But I didn't hire you. And I'm not going to."

"Why not?"

"You were right. Whoever wrote that note

58

is crazy. Or mean. Or both." She put her ballet bag inside her backpack. Melody had ballet lessons every Tuesday. "So I'm going to forget about it. If there's a note today, I'll throw it out."

"That's smart," I said. I didn't really need a case right now anyway. Baseball practice kept me busy enough.

Today wasn't as cold as yesterday. It was sunny, but there was still a little snow on the ground. Jack told me practice was inside again. I ran to the gym.

Danger

The afternoon brought a chill. The remaining snow was now a thin crust. I crunched home. Brian's apple tree was bare and brown again.

There was a note taped to my porch door:

59

"I'm over at Brian's. Come dance with us. —M."

Maybe Melody was teaching Brian ballet.

Ballet was hard. All that toe pointing and kicking. But Brian might like it. He liked things you'd never expect.

I dropped my backpack inside the porch and went next door. I knocked.

No one answered. And the door was unlocked. I stuck my head in.

The music was on loud.

Marissa and Brian and Melody were dancing in the living room. To a CD player—not YouTube. The furniture was pushed aside.

They smiled at me. And kept dancing. Goofy dancing, with their arms flying all over. Nothing like ballet.

This was my kind of dancing. I joined in.

Brian jumped on the couch. Marissa didn't stop him. I had never seen a babysitter like Marissa.

An alarm went off.

"What's that?" asked Melody.

Marissa looked at her watch. She pushed something. The alarm stopped. I had never seen an alarm watch before. She did a thumbs-up to Brian.

Brian turned off the music. He did a thumbs-up to Marissa.

Marissa pushed the furniture back in place. She did another thumbs-up.

Brian straightened the couch cushions. He did another thumbs-up.

I had never seen Brian so cooperative.

Three surprises in a row. But a sleuth is never shaken by surprises. "Is your mother due home now, Brian?"

"How did you know?"

"Even I figured that out," said Melody.

"See you later." I headed for the back door.

"Wait, Sly." Melody caught up. "I'm coming

with you." She put her mouth to my ear. "I got another note."

Oh, no. But she was smiling. Maybe she was holding back tears. I forced a smile too.

When we got inside my porch, I said, "Show me."

But Melody already had the note out.

This one was short. I read:

I looked at Melody.

"This one is good, right?" said Melody.

"Why do you say that?"

"It's got a smiley face. Smiley faces are good. I just don't know what *sole* means."

"It means alone."

"Don't be dumb, Sly. I know that. Do you think the person is asking to be alone with me?"

"I don't know." I frowned. I didn't like this

one bit. Despite the smiley face. Who would want to be alone with Melody besides Jack? But Jack probably didn't even know the word *sole*.

Before, I thought the note-writer was crazy. Now I thought the note-writer might be dangerous.

Spelling

In our school when the bell rings, we change classes. So on Wednesday, whenever that bell rang, I ran to Melody's cubby. Plus I passed Melody's cubby four more times. On the way to the bathroom. On the way to lunch. On the way to recess. And once just to pass it. A sleuth must be persistent. That's what my father says.

No one went near Melody's cubby.

After school, I said to Melody, "No note today, right?"

"Right," said Melody. She sounded disappointed. How dumb. That note-writer was creepy.

I grabbed my jacket and ran outside to baseball practice. The ground was muddy. But real players don't care about a little mud.

On Thursday at the first bell, I ran to Melody's cubby.

"You're lurking," came a voice.

I jumped.

Kate stood behind me.

"I'm not lurking."

"You slink along this hall a lot. I saw you yesterday. I saw you this morning before school. That's called lurking. You're on a case."

"No I'm not." That was the truth. After all, Melody hadn't hired me. "Bye." I walked away.

If Kate had noticed me, maybe the note-writer had noticed me. Maybe that's why there were no more notes.

I'd never discover who the note-writer was this way.

I stayed far from Melody's cubby the rest of the morning. At lunch I sat with her. "No note yet, right?" I said hopefully.

"Right," said Melody. Her voice was definitely sad.

But I couldn't feel sorry for her. I was happy. Maybe the note-writer had quit.

No such luck. After school, Melody stood in front of her cubby. With a note in her hand.

But she was smiling. "Hey, Sly, do you think I'm sassy?"

"Sassy?" I punched my fist into the web of my baseball mitt. I wanted to soften that part.

Coach told us to catch in the web, not the palm. "Who uses a word like *sassy*?"

"It's a good word. It means you have energy and spunk. And you're cute."

"It might mean energy and spunk," I said. "But it has nothing to do with cute."

"That's not true. You call people sassy when you think they're cute. Look." She held up the note, facing me.

I saw one word: *sassi*.

"Your hands are in the way. Is there only one word?"

"No, there's more. But it's private."

Private? What was private between best friends? The note-writer wanted to be alone with Melody. And now there were private words. "*Sassy* has a *y*, not an *i*," I said. "What a bad speller."

"There are more important things than spelling," said Melody. She folded the note

66

into her pocket. Then she peeled today's orange.

"Like baseball practice," I said.

"You can be pretty self-centered," said Melody.

Those were rough words from a best friend. I punched my fist into my mitt again. "There's no practice tomorrow. Coach likes Fridays off. Want to play after school?"

"Kate already asked me."

I ran to baseball practice feeling blue.

But the ground was dryer today. And the sun was bright.

We had a great practice. I almost hit the ball. Twice.

Rocks and Chocolate

Friday was a pretty good day. I had hummus and pita bread for lunch. Hummus is a tasty bean mash. Almost as good as peanut butter. It's from far away. The Middle East, I think. Mrs. Olsen made it. She even made the bread. She brought it over last night.

Other parts of the day were fun too. In science Princess showed us rocks. Her cousin bought them at the Academy of Natural Sciences. One was Ordovician. One was Silurian. One was Devonian. That means they were old. Over 400 million years old. They were found here in Pennsylvania. Left from when it was under a sea.

I never knew Pennsylvania used to be under a sea.

Princess's cousin is a rock fiend. She wants to become a paleontologist and study rocks as a job. The rocks had fossils in them. She was going back to the museum to buy more.

So school was good. Or good enough.

But walking home wasn't. I walked alone. I didn't want to look up.

I didn't want to see Melody walk off with Kate.

I didn't want to see Princess walk off with her cousin.

Jack jumped out of nowhere. He has a habit of doing that. Noah was behind him.

"Has Melody said anything yet?" asked Jack.

"About the oranges?"

"Yes."

"She likes them."

Jack grinned. "Great. So, she'll go to the school Valentine's party with me."

"Well, I don't know about that, Jack."

"What? Why do you say that?"

"Oranges are one thing. Parties are another.

They have nothing to do with each other."

"But she likes the oranges. So she'll like me for giving them to her. So she'll go to the party with me. It's logical."

It was a good thing Jack wasn't a sleuth. That kind of logic would get him nowhere. "I hope so, Jack. Ask her."

"I will. And Princess will go with Noah."

"Oh, yeah?" I looked at Noah. "Did she like the flourless chocolate cake?"

Noah gave a small smile.

"Everyone liked it," said Jack. "Princess and her sister Angel, and her parents, and her cousin Lucia, and her aunt. They all ate it."

"How do you know?"

"I was there. I was helping Mr. Monti mist the orange trees. I heard the whole thing. I even got a piece."

"Tell her what they said," mumbled Noah.

"*Cioccolato!*" yelled Jack.

What did that mean? A man across the street stopped and stared at us. "Don't yell," I said. "People are looking."

"But that's what they did. They ran around the house yelling, '*Cioccolato.*' And other things too. But that's the only word I caught."

"What do you mean, the only word you caught?"

"I don't speak Italian. Or not much. I've picked up a few words, from Mr. Monti. But anyone can figure out what *cioccolato* means."

I was still confused.

Noah mouthed the word *chocolate*.

Oh, of course. *Cioccolato* was Italian for *chocolate*. It seemed obvious now. You just had to pronounce all the vowels in the English word. Even the silent one at the end.

But somehow you had to know to turn that silent *e* to an *o*. How?

Maybe I was bad at foreign languages.

Party on the Field

Saturday morning the phone woke me. I sat up in bed. The sun was bright. It was a perfect day.

"Sly!" my mother called up the stairs. "Get the phone, sweetie. It's for you."

I went to the hall phone. "Hello?"

"Hi, Sly. It's Princess."

"Hi, Princess."

"Want to play?"

"With you and your cousin?"

"Just me. Lucia's sick."

"That's too bad."

"No it isn't. I don't like to be mean. But I need some time off. She complains that I don't answer her. But I give her all my attention. It's driving me crazy. Want to meet me at the school field?"

"The field?"

"Noah says it's the best place to practice baseball."

Noah said all that? Wow.

I bet Princess was pretty bad. But any practice helped. "That's a great idea."

"See you in a half hour?"

"Sure."

"And, Sly, do you have an extra mitt?"

"I have an old one."

"Could you bring it? Please? I don't have one."

Yup. Princess would be bad. "Sure. Bye."

I dressed fast. Then I gobbled a bowl of cereal. I had just put my jacket on when the phone rang. This time I answered.

"Hello?"

"Hi, Sly." It was Melody. She sounded breathless. "Want to take Pong for a walk with me?" Pong is Melody's puppy.

"I'm going to the school field."

"What for?"

"To practice baseball."

"You can't practice baseball all alone. I'll walk Pong fast and then come with you. I like to pitch." Melody hated to pitch. She was just being nice. She felt guilty for dumping me yesterday.

"Thanks. But you don't have to do that."

"Yes I do."

"Princess is coming," I said.

"Oh. Well, I want to come too. Kate called. She's coming over. And I can't take being alone with her again. So we're both coming. Don't say no, Sly. I need you. Bye." She hung up.

By the time I got to the field, Princess was already there. With Lucia.

"This is my cousin Lucia," said Princess.

"Hello," I said. "I'm Sly."

"*Piacere*," mumbled Lucia. That must have meant something good, because she smiled.

I smiled back. "I thought she was sick," I said to Princess.

"She was. And she's shy—because of English. But it turns out she loves baseball. She says it's the great American sport. And it's sunny. Lucia loves the sun. So when she heard why I was coming, she got out of bed."

"Hi, everyone."

We turned to look.

Kate and Melody ran up. With Pong on a leash.

This was turning out to be a party.

Rhythm

Sunday morning was cloudy. But the afternoon got sunny. Just right for baseball. Maybe I'd head over to Princess's. Yesterday had been fun. It turned out Lucia was a great pitcher. I could learn from her.

And she didn't complain or act shy. She kept yelling, "*Brava.*" The first time I thought it was odd. What was brave about baseball? But Princess said it was a compliment—for when you made a good play.

Lucia made us all feel good.

I put my stuff in my pack and went out the porch door.

"Play with me!" Brian came running over.

"I'm going to practice. For baseball."

"I love baseball."

Taxi walked over and rubbed around Brian's legs. Her tail stuck straight up. Brian played with the tip of it.

"Do you even know what baseball is, Brian?"

"You bash balls with a stick."

"You have to be able to catch too."

"I can't catch," said Brian. I knew that, of course. He looked at me. His eyes got big and sad. He could be almost as dramatic as Melody.

Well, hey. If Lucia could be encouraging, so could I. "Throwing's good enough for today, though. Go get a ball, Brian."

"Yay!" Brian searched under his apple tree. He came back with a big blue one.

"Okay, here's how it works. You throw the ball at my house."

"The house can't catch."

"Right. But throw as hard as you can. When it bounces off, I'll run after it. I have to get it within three seconds."

"Why?"

"That's what Coach wants."

"My music teacher makes us count too. That's rhythm. She loves rhythm."

Brian threw the ball. It hit the window. It was a good thing the ball was rubber.

I fielded it. "This time don't hit the window. Just the side."

"You lost."

"What?"

"Five seconds." Brian wound up his arm. He threw the ball. It went up over his head. It caught in the maple tree.

I don't like heights. I don't climb trees unless I have to.

I got the rake from the garage. I batted the ball free. I handed it to Brian.

"You lost."

"Brian, you threw it in the tree."

"A million thirty hundred seconds. Rhythm, Sly. Didn't you pay attention in music class?"

"Hey, Sly. Hey, Brian." It was Melody. "I need to talk to you, Sly."

"Noooo!" screamed Brian. "Sly never plays with me anymore. All she does is baseball practice."

I don't like it when Brian screams. But he missed me. I put my hand on his head. "We can talk and play ball at the same time."

"I've got a better idea," said Melody. "Let's paint while we talk."

"I love painting," said Brian.

Good. I was tired of losing.

Beads

We sat on the floor, all ready to paint.

I handed a piece of paper to Melody.

"No thanks."

"What? You said we should paint."

"You and Brian can paint on paper. I'm going to paint on . . ." Melody took a bag out of her pocket. She gently spilled the contents on the floor. ". . . beads."

Brian picked up a bead. "I love clay."

I stared at the beads. "You made clay beads without me."

Melody took the bead from Brian. "I know, Sly. I'm sorry."

"We always make beads together," I said.

"I didn't want to hurt your feelings."

"Why would making beads together hurt my feelings?"

Melody sighed. "Something good happened to me. And it didn't happen to you. And I didn't want you to feel bad."

"You made beads without me because something good happened to you?"

"They're for a necklace. I have to paint these beads really pretty."

This was too confusing. "If you didn't want to make the beads with me, why would you paint them with me?"

"Because I realized I needed to talk to you about it."

I shook my head. "Start over, Melody. Start at the beginning."

"Okay." Melody gave a small smile. "I've been dying to tell you, really." She giggled. "I got invited to the school Valentine's party."

Was that all? I smiled big.

Melody grinned back. "I should have known

you'd be happy for me. We're best friends, after all." She wiggled on her bottom.

I had to know if Jack's logic was right. "Was it because of the oranges?"

"What are you talking about?"

Oops. "Who invited you?"

"I don't know."

"What do you mean you don't know?"

"I'm hiring you to find out." Melody took a piece of paper out of her pocket. "You need to see the whole note—not just the middle." She spread it on the floor.

I read:

"This is an invitation to the Valentine's party?"

"What else could it be? He's asking me to come. So it's got to be the party. But he still didn't write his name. Find out who he is, Sly."

Vowels

I dialed Jack's number.

"Yes."

"I didn't ask a question yet, Jack."

"Sly? What do you want?"

"Did you invite Melody?"

"No."

"Have you been leaving notes in her cubby?"

"No."

"Bye, Jack." I hung up.

I went back into the kitchen to Melody. "Go home and get all the notes, Melody."

"I have them. I always carry them." She put them on the table.

"There's only three. What happened to the first one?"

"It made no sense. Remember? It didn't even use real words. So I threw it out. He must have been nervous at first."

I arranged the notes in the order they came

in. I frowned. They were as odd now as they were the first time I saw them.

Brian stood beside me. He put his finger on the first note. "I know that word: *me.*" He screwed up his mouth. "*Pizzz-zzza.* What's that mean?"

"Pizza."

"Oh, yeah. *Do-ve*? What's that mean?"

"It's not *do-ve*," said Melody. "It's *dove.* The *e* is silent."

"Wait!" I yelped. The way Brian said that, it reminded me of something. Brian had talked about rhythm before. "What if Brian's way of saying it is right?" I read all the words again, saying each vowel. And now I knew what it reminded me of: the way Jack said *cioccolato*, for chocolate.

I used the phone in the kitchen. It didn't matter if Melody heard me now.

"Hello?"

"Hi, Princess. When did Lucia come to town?"

"Last Thursday."

"Does Lucia know where your cubby is?"

"Yes. She walked to school with me last Friday morning. I showed it to her."

"Did she look inside it?"

Melody's cubby was lined with ballet pictures. No one could mistake it.

"No, I just pointed to it as we passed."

"Is there a word *do-ve* in Italian?"

"Yes. It means 'where.'"

"Bye, Princess."

"Wait. Are you okay, Sly?"

"Sure. Why?"

"You sound crazy."

"I'm not. I have to go now. Bye."

I could have just asked Princess about all the words in the notes. But that would be too easy. A sleuth gets paid. So a sleuth has to do a little work, after all. Plus the work is the fun part.

I went to the computer. Melody stood on

one side of me. Brian stood on the other. I found an Italian dictionary. I translated each note.

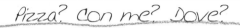

Pizza? With me? Where?

☺ sun.

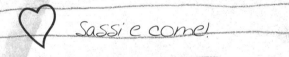

♡ rocks. And how!

"These notes are in Italian," I announced.

"I can see that," said Melody.

"And they're not inviting you to the Valentine's party."

"I can see that too." Melody's face fell.

"But don't worry. You're still going to get invited."

"How do you know?"

"I just do."

Whose Cubby

This was the fastest case I'd ever had. Lucia wrote those notes. They were for Princess. She walked to our school and left the notes in a cubby. She just confused Melody's cubby for Princess's.

The clues weren't perfectly clear, because the notes didn't make sense on their own. You needed to know more to understand them. But I knew enough.

Note 1: Pizza? With me? Where?

First, all Lucia wanted to eat was pizza. So

she was asking Princess to eat pizza with her. She must have asked where because she didn't know our town. We only have one pizza joint.

Note 2: ☺ sun.

This note was easy. It came on Wednesday. Lucia loves the sun. The sun came out Wednesday.

Note 3: ♡ rocks. And how!

This was pretty easy, too. Lucia loves rocks. Princess had shown us rocks she'd bought at the museum.

Melody was sad at first. But she got happy because Jack finally invited her to the Valentine's party. She gave me three baseball cards as payment for my job. She collects them, even though she doesn't play.

Lucia was happy. She thought Princess was ignoring her notes. But now she knew Princess had never seen them.

Brian was happy. I gave him one of the baseball cards. After all, his words broke the case. You had to pay attention to rhythm. Different languages have different rhythms. Once I understood that, it all came together.

And I was really happy. Instead of creepy notes, they were just Italian notes.

And, hey, a language was a code. So breaking this case was decoding the notes.

Two coding cases in a row. And both started out kind of scary. But both ended up fine. I liked code mysteries.

Case #3:

Sly and the

Baseball Beat

Lucia

Baseball practice on Monday was crowded.

Princess came. That I expected.

Kate came. That was a surprise.

Melody came. That was a shock.

Lucia came. That knocked me over.

I should have been happy. But I wasn't. Baseball was my thing. I loved it. These girls didn't. I wanted to be on the team. And I didn't need extra competition.

Coach let them all stay. Even Lucia. He

smiled. "The more people at practice, the better," he said.

Coach divided us into two teams. Lucia was on the other team.

The first two batters struck out. That was dumb. The balls went high. The catcher couldn't even reach them. If they hadn't swung, they would have walked. But it was okay with me. That wasn't my team.

Lucia was next. She swung the bat over her head. I never saw anyone swing like that. She hit the ball. She made it to second base.

The next batter swung and missed.

"Strike one," called Coach.

Lucia waved to the batter.

The batter stared at her. A ball went whizzing over his head.

"Ball one," called Coach.

Lucia stole third base. I'd never stolen a base before. I'd never even tried. Lucia waved to the batter.

The batter frowned at her and looked at the pitcher. Too late. A ball whizzed over his head.

"Ball two," called Coach.

If Lucia kept distracting that batter, he was going to walk.

Lucia waved wildly to the batter. He wouldn't look at her. He swung at the ball. The ball went flying into the backstop.

"Strike two," called Coach.

The catcher fumbled with the ball.

Lucia stole home.

Lucia stole home! No one steals home. I mean, Ty Cobb stole home. But Ty Cobb was a great player. A legend.

The next ball flew high. The batter swung.

"Strike three," called Coach.

Our team was up.

Lucia was pitcher. Her balls went straight over the plate. At chest level. They should have been easy to hit. But they were fast. She struck out three batters in a row.

Tomorrow I wanted to be on Lucia's team.

Challenge

Lucia's team won.

We zipped up our jackets to go home.

Jasper came over. A group of boys stood behind him. "Where did you learn to play like that?" he asked Lucia.

Lucia looked at Princess. Princess translated. Lucia answered.

"What's wrong with her?" asked Jasper.

"She's from Italy," said Kate.

"Weird," said Jasper. "It sounds like messed-up Spanish."

"Do you want to know the answer or not?" asked Princess.

"Yes," said Jasper.

"All her friends love American baseball. They watch videos. They play on the weekends. Italy has a national team, you know."

"Weird," said Jasper. "Well, I'm glad she's here. We'll win this year."

"She's leaving on Friday," said Princess.

"Aw." Jasper shook his head. "Then it's just you. And all of you are lousy."

Kate put her hands on her hips. "All of who?"

"All of you. You girls."

"That's what I thought you meant," said Kate. "You're uneducated."

Jasper blinked. "Uneducated?"

I blinked too. What was Kate talking about?

"Girls and boys are equal. Anyone who doesn't know that is uneducated," said Kate. "You need to be educated."

"Huh?" said Jasper.

"We challenge you to a baseball game. Girls against boys," said Kate.

Melody and Princess and I stared at her. Lucia just looked from one face to another.

"You're on," said Jasper. "This weekend."

"No," said Kate. "Thursday after school."

"But that Italian girl's still here on Thursday."

"She's only one," said Kate. "What? Are you afraid one girl can beat a whole boys' team?"

"Never!" said Jasper. "Thursday. Right here on this field!"

Everyone Agrees

"You just spoke for all of us," said Melody. "You didn't even ask."

That's exactly what I wanted to say.

"Don't whine," said Kate. This was extra-bossy, even for Kate.

"What if the other girls don't agree?" asked Princess.

"We'll make them agree. Melody, you call Lacey and Kirsten. Princess, you call Sola and Jennifer. Sly, you call Emily and Chaundra."

I put my hands on my hips. Now I looked

just like Kate. "That doesn't leave anyone for you to call."

"I'm the organizer. I have enough to do. I have to make my mother buy us a new mitt for our catcher. We need the best."

"New mitts aren't best," I said. "They aren't broken in. We want a used mitt. They're supple."

"Supple?" said Kate.

"Supple," I said. "That's baseball talk."

Melody stepped up beside me. "Sly knows baseball." Good old Melody.

"All right, all right. No new mitt. But I have other things to do. I have to go organize." Kate ran off.

When I got home I called Emily and Chaundra. They agreed. I phoned Melody and Princess. Everyone they had called agreed too.

The game was on.

At a real game like this, everyone would play hard. And everyone would notice who played good.

I just hoped I wouldn't be the worst player.

I was so nervous, I couldn't do my home-work.

I walked over to Brian's.

"Sly! You came to play."

"I came to dance."

"Do you hate baseball now?"

"No."

"Oh. But you still came anyway. Dance!"

We danced the afternoon away.

Bathrooms

I stood in the water fountain line in the caf-eteria.

Pete stood in front of me. He muttered.

"What'd you say?" I asked.

Pete jumped. He looked at me as though I had cooties. He drank and ran off.

I drank and sat back down at my seat.

Mrs. Kandybowicz came into the cafeteria. She works in the principal's office. We call her Kandy behind her back. But Kandy never has anything sweet to say.

"Silvia?"

Uh-oh. Kandy was talking to me. That was strange enough. But it was even stranger that she used my real name.

"Yes, Mrs. Kandybowicz?"

"Principal wants to see you." That's how Kandy talked. She said *principal* like we said *coach*—as though it was a name.

"Now?"

"Yes."

I shoved the rest of my sandwich into my mouth. I followed Kandy to the principal's office.

"Hello, Sly." Principal Ramirez used my nickname. And she didn't look mad.

"Hello."

"Have a seat, please."

I sat down.

"We have a little problem. Stuart brought it to my attention."

Stuart is our school custodian. He's nice. He whistles. And he likes us. But he really can't tell us apart. He doesn't see well.

I wondered if Stuart saw someone do something wrong. Maybe he thought the person was me.

"It's a little delicate. It's in the boys' bathrooms."

"I never go in the boys' bathrooms," I said.

"Of course you don't. But someone has been writing on the stalls."

"I don't write on stalls."

"Of course you don't. But we don't understand what this person wrote. And we're worried about what it might mean. So . . ."

"So?"

"I'm hiring you. As a sleuth."

"You know about my detective agency?"

"Everyone knows. I want you to find out

who's writing in the bathrooms. And what it means."

"Do I have to go in the boys' bathrooms?"

"I'm not sure. I guess I could copy the graffiti for you."

I didn't like the idea of Principal Ramirez having to go in the boys' bathrooms. But I didn't like the idea of me having to go in there worse. "I have to think about this," I said.

"Why?"

"I always think about my cases."

"That's wise," said Principal Ramirez. "How long do you need?"

"Till tomorrow."

Barks and Purrs

At baseball practice more people than ever showed up. Word had gotten around about the challenge game.

Coach scratched his head. He smiled. "It's great to see so many newcomers."

"They're here to practice for the challenge game," said Jasper. "On Thursday. Boys versus girls."

Coach stopped smiling. "Does everyone want this?"

Some people said yes. Some people kept quiet. No one said no.

I wanted to say no. I stepped forward. Kate pinched me. She whispered, "Solidarity."

"What does that mean?" I whispered back.

"I'll tell you later."

"Why don't we break up another way?" said Coach. "You know, something other than girls versus boys?"

"It's got to be girls versus boys," said Jasper.

"And all of you agree?" Coach looked around at us.

No one said anything.

Coach threw up his hands. "If that's what you

want. But once tryouts are over, the real team will never do it this way." Then he clapped. "I guess it'll build up the spirit of competition. Okay. For the first half of practice, we all train together. Then boys can use that end of the field." He pointed. "And girls can use that end." He pointed. "I'll go back and forth between you, giving pointers."

So that's what we did.

When Coach wasn't giving pointers, Lucia was. Through Princess.

Lucia said you ran faster if you pretended a big dog was after you.

She said you caught better if you didn't close your eyes.

She said you hit better if you watched the ball.

These were all pointers I knew. Except the one about the dog.

It helped. We did better today.

Whatever Lucia said, Kate repeated it. Over and over. Once, after Kate said a rule, Kirsten walked behind her and barked. Everyone laughed.

"What are you doing?" said Kate.

"Acting like you."

"I'm not a dog," said Kate.

"Then stop barking at us," said Sola.

"You need it," said Kate. "Who else is going to whip you into shape?" But she quieted down a little after that.

Afterward, I walked home alone. Melody

wasn't at practice. It was Tuesday, and Tuesday is ballet day.

I sat on my back steps. I picked up Taxi and petted her. "I'm worried, Taxi. I might not make the team."

Taxi purred.

"And the principal wants me to take a case. A bathroom case."

Taxi purred louder. I forgot. Taxi likes bathrooms. She likes to turn over the trash and search for toys. Taxi has odd ideas about what makes a good toy. Probably all cats do. Taxi would want me to take this case. Probably any cat would.

But I didn't want to.

It felt good that the principal came to me for help. But bathrooms? I could imagine people calling me the stinky sleuth.

Nope, this was a bad case.

I put Taxi down and went over to Brian's. Marissa was there. The three of us danced.

Just Drawings

The cafeteria was quieter than normal on Wednesday. Especially the boys. A whole table of them seemed to be muttering softly. Just like Pete had at the water fountain the day before. It was odd.

And the quiet made it worse when Kandy came in again. Everyone watched her call me over.

I followed her to the principal's office.

"Hello, Sly. Have a seat."

"I can't take the case, Principal Ramirez," I said. "I'm sorry."

"I'm even sorrier, Sly." Principal Ramirez made a little *tsk*. "It's gotten worse. Yesterday, after I talked with you, Stuart cleaned off the stall walls. Then, in the afternoon, the graffiti was back up again."

I tried to look sympathetic.

"He cleaned it off. This morning, there it was again. But a new symbol today."

A symbol? What did that mean? What kind of symbol? But I didn't ask.

"Could I just show you what was there yesterday?"

"You drew it?"

"Actually, I had Stuart photograph it." Principal Ramirez handed me a photo.

I saw a circle with two dots in it and a half circle attached to the left side. An arrow pointed at the little half circle.

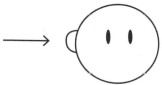

"Do you know what it means?" asked Principal Ramirez.

"No."

She handed me another photo. "This is what Stuart washed off this morning."

I saw two straight vertical lines, with two more going off at a slant to the right. An arrow pointed at the lines on the right.

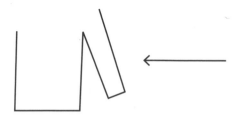

"It makes no sense to me," I said.

"I was afraid of that." Principal Ramirez looked sad. "Okay, Sly. Thanks for your help."

I didn't help. And we both knew it. I hate it when people thank you for doing nothing. Now I felt guilty. I should try to help Principal Ramirez.

But I didn't know what those drawings could mean. Besides, it was just drawings. Who cared?

Doom

Wednesday's baseball practice was a repeat of Tuesday's. Except Melody was there. So at least I wasn't the only one who didn't hit the ball.

After practice the boys ran off. Muttering again. What had gotten into them?

But Kate shouted, "Huddle." It was about the hundredth time she'd shouted at us that afternoon. "Huddle! Huddle!"

"I thought 'huddle' was for football," said Emily.

Kate frowned. "Sly, can you say 'huddle' in baseball?"

I didn't know. But I hated to admit it to Kate. "The person in charge can say whatever she wants."

"Right," said Kate. "Huddle!"

"I thought Lucia was in charge," said Princess. "She's the best player."

"I'm the one who organized the game," said Kate. "Huddle!"

The girls crowded together.

"Tomorrow we have to kick their you-know-whats," said Kate.

"Their whats?" said Lacey.

"You-know-whats," said Melody. She giggled. Everyone giggled.

"So eat a big dinner," said Kate.

"What if I'm not hungry?" said Kirsten.

"Get hungry," said Kate. "And go to bed early."

"What if I have a lot of homework?" said Sola.

"Do it sloppy and fast," said Kate. "And, listen, this is the most important part."

"What if I'm tired of listening to you?" said Jennifer.

Everyone giggled.

I felt sort of bad for Kate. But if you're bossy, that's what happens.

"Do you want to win or not?" said Kate.

"I want to win," said Chaundra. "My brother's on the boys' team."

"That's the spirit," said Kate. "Beat your brother. Okay, now, the most important thing is to think positive. Go to sleep convinced we'll win."

Everyone separated. I turned around to join Melody. And there was Principal Ramirez.

"Sly, may I talk to you a minute, please?"

Melody's eyes got huge. "I'll wait for you."

"It might be a while, Melody," said Principal Ramirez. "Don't worry. I'll see that Sly gets home."

"Ooo-ooo. Look who's in trouble," I heard someone whisper.

"Sly's not in trouble," said Principal Ramirez. "I just need her help."

No one said anything else. The girls left.

"I'm sorry about the rumors," said Principal Ramirez.

I just looked at her.

"That symbol got drawn again this afternoon. So Stuart washed it off after school. I just went in—just now—for one last check." Principal Ramirez shook her head sadly. "There's a new symbol."

"A new symbol?"

"Yes."

It wasn't there when school ended. But it was there now. Wow. "Who's been around since school got out?"

"Only the kids going out for baseball."

Double wow.

"Please, Sly. Will you come look in the bathroom with me?"

I followed Principal Ramirez inside. What if somebody saw?

I marched. Onward, to my doom.

A Vulnerable Age

There were three stalls in this bathroom. All of them had a drawing. The same drawing. It was a half circle, sitting on one side of a straight line. An arrow pointed to the part of the line that stuck out beyond the half circle.

"I don't get it," I said.

"Think about it, will you?" asked Principal Ramirez.

"Have you asked any of the boys?"

"That's the first thing I did. I asked Jack and Chris and Mario and Jasper and Carlo." She counted off on her fingers. Brian did that sometimes. It made me like Principal Ramirez even more. "Some of them had no idea what it was. Some of them said they couldn't say."

"Just like that? Those words: 'I can't say'?"

"Exactly," said Principal Ramirez. "As though it was a secret."

"Did Jack say he didn't know what it was?"

"Yes. He's the one who suggested I hire you, in fact."

"Did Jasper say he couldn't say?"

"Yes. How did you guess?"

"I have to think about it before I say more."

"Please do, Sly. Something's going on with the boys. And this is a vulnerable age. It's important that I know what's happening. And that I stop anything bad before it becomes serious."

Something was going on with the boys, all

right. Their muttering made me a little edgy. "I decided. I'm taking your case."

"Good. Now I'll drive you home."

"That's okay," I said. "It's not far. If I run, I can catch up with Melody."

"All right. If you're sure."

I ran down the hall and out the door.

"Cheater!"

I turned around.

No one was there.

Cheater? I had thought of a lot of insults people might say if they knew I went in a boys' bathroom. But *cheater* wasn't one of them.

Arrows

I ran the rest of the way home. Melody was nowhere in sight. It must have taken longer with Principal Ramirez than I'd thought.

When I got in the back door, my mother
was waiting for me.

"How are you, Sly?"

"Fine." I dropped my backpack and sank
onto a kitchen chair.

Mother put a bowl of orange slices in front
of me. "Melody called." She sat down across
from me. "She wanted to know if you were
home yet. She said the principal kept you late."
Mother's face was worried.

"I'm not in trouble, Mother."

"What's going on?"

"It's a case."

"A case? A detective case?"

"The boys are writing crazy things on the
bathroom walls. Principal Ramirez wants me
to find out why."

"Oh. Well, that's nice then, I guess."

"If I can figure it out."

"I'm sure you can. You always do."

It's good to have a mother who believes in you.

I took out a piece of paper and drew the things that were on the bathroom walls.

There was an arrow in each one. Beyond that, they didn't seem to have anything in common.

Jack played soccer, not baseball. And Jack didn't know what those symbols meant.

But Jasper did.

And the third one appeared today. After baseball practice. Only the boys who went out for the team had used the bathroom then.

The drawings had something to do with baseball.

Drawing Lessons

"You forgot." Brian appeared at my side.

"What did I forget?"

"To come play with me."

"I can't play every day, Brian."

"You can play now."

"I'm working on a case now."

"No, you're not. You're drawing. Bad. People need two ears. See?" Brian added an ear.

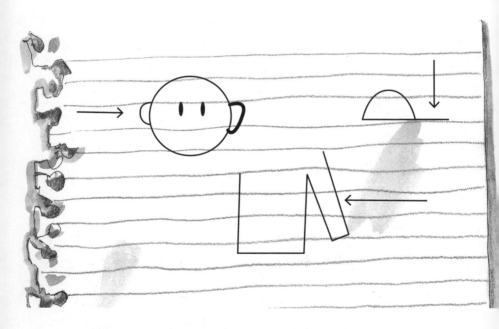

Hey. With two ears, those two dots in the middle did look like eyes. Maybe it was a face, looking at us. With an arrow pointing at the right ear.

"What's this a drawing of, Brian?" I pointed at the other two drawings.

"You need drawing lessons, Sly. I could help you."

"You already did. Here, draw anything you want. I have to use the computer."

"For YouTube?"

"No."

"Then I can come with you."

"Okay."

Brian and I went to the computer. There sure were a lot of baseball sites. And many of them talked about signals.

I knew a lot of signals from baseball last year. Coach hadn't talked about them yet this year. But I remembered. And I remembered right.

Pulling on your right ear meant: Steal a base.

Touching your right hand to your left arm meant: Take a pitch.

Touching the visor of your cap meant: Bunt.

There were other signals too. But those three were enough.

The drawings in the boys' bathroom were baseball signals, for sure.

The Key

I telephoned Princess.

"Hello?"

"Hi, Princess. Will you please ask Lucia if she knows about baseball signals?"

"Okay. Just a minute."

We were back in the kitchen now. I watched Brian draw as I waited. He made a duck. The baseball cap was now part of the duck's head.

"Sly?" said Princess.

"Yes."

"Lucia knows all about signals."

"Why didn't she use them with us?"

"Wait." I could hear Princess talking in Italian to Lucia. "She hates signals."

"Why?"

"Well, for example, someone might tell you to take a pitch. But Lucia loves to swing. And hit the ball hard. She hates to take a pitch.

She'd rather hit the ball, any ball, no matter how bad it is. So signals aren't any fun for a good player, like her."

I understood. Signals were about strategy. Playing without signals was about physical skill. I liked both in my games. But some people liked only the physical part.

"Thanks, Princess."

"Wait. Are you in trouble, Sly?"

"No."

"But I saw you go off with the principal."

"I'm on a case."

"Cool."

I opened the school directory. I telephoned Jasper.

"Hello?"

"Hi, Jasper. This is Sly."

"What do you want?"

"Do you think the boys could beat the girls just on physical skill?"

"I don't know what you're talking about."

"Do you think you need signals to beat us?" I asked.

"It's smart to use signals."

"That's what I thought," I said.

"Signals are fair," said Jasper. "Don't act like they're a cheat. We work hard to memorize them." He hung up.

Memorize them. Sometimes when I memorize things, I say them under my breath.

All that muttering.

I went back to the Internet. I read more about baseball signals. The coach picks a key signal. It might be touching the cap visor, for example. Then in a game, he'll make many signals in a row. Fast. But the only signal that matters is the first one after the key. So if the coach does this series:

> *Right hand to left arm*
> *Pull on right ear*

Left hand to right arm
Touch cap visor
Pull on right ear
Right hand to left arm

that means the coach is telling the player to steal a base. Because the first signal after the key is pulling on the right ear.

The boys were writing the key signal of the day.

And touching the cap visor was tomorrow's key signal. The key for the big challenge game.

That's why someone had called me a cheater.

Rhythm

Principal Ramirez was happy when she found out the drawings were baseball signals.

She had Stuart put up chalkboards in the

boys' bathrooms. For messages. But she made an announcement that all messages had to be good.

I wondered who would decide what was good.

Principal Ramirez paid me with a detention pass. So if I ever got a detention, I could get out of it. I have never had a detention. I don't plan on getting one. But I can give my pass to someone else if I want. So it's good payment.

At the start of the challenge game on Thursday, I announced that the girls' team knew the boys' team's key signal. I am not a cheater.

The boys groaned. They changed their key signal right then and there. And they used signals anyway. But they kept getting confused about what the new key was. They lost.

Only by one run, though.

And Lucia scored all but one of the girls' runs. So without her, the boys would have beat us.

Lucia was happy. Before she left for Italy, she told Princess she loved America. But she said she was glad to leave because Pennsylvania in winter is too cold.

The girls had a party to celebrate. On Friday. They crowned Kate queen. Of nothing. But at least she was queen.

Kate was happy. She said her crown was a symbol of solidarity. Girls should stick up for other girls when boys were uneducated. She said solidarity was better than being invited to the Valentine's party by a boy. Princess could go with Noah. And Melody could go with Jack. Who cared? She said her mother thinks we're too young to go as couples anyway.

I said we should go with Jennifer and Sola. No one had invited them either.

Kate got even happier. She said I now understood solidarity. So on Saturday, we four girls went to the Valentine's party. It was fun.

And I was happier than anyone. I explained it all to Taxi. This was my third code case. Baseball signals are a code, after all. And all my cases had something to do with rhythm.

The Case of the Song Beat was about rapping rhythm.

The Case of the Word Beat was about recognizing Italian words by pronouncing all the vowels. If you say *dove* with a silent "e" at the end, you only have one beat. But if you say it with two vowels, you have two beats. So the rhythm changes.

The Case of the Baseball Beat was about the key signal. The key might come at any point in a series of signals. There was no fixed rhythm. And that was important—that's what kept the key secret.

The funny thing is, rhythm is also important to poetry. And poetry is always on my mind when I sleuth. That's because somehow all my cases turn out poetic. My pet cases rhymed. My sports cases had alliteration. My food cases had plays on words. And these code cases all have a beat.

Sleuthing is the most poetic occupation I know. Besides being a poet, that is.

Be sure to crack the case with Sly in these books!